WARNING!

SCAREDY SQUIRREL INSISTS
THAT THIS BOOK NOT BE READ
IN BATHROOMS.

READER SECURITY QUIZ

1. I HOLD BOOKS WITH...

HANDS ☐ (1 point)

SHARP CLAWS ☐ (0 points)

SLIMY TENTACLES ☐ (0 points)

2. SQUIRRELS ARE...

OVERRATED ☐ (0 points)

FUN TO CHASE ☐ (-1 point)

LOVABLE RODENTS ☐ (1 point)

3. I SMELL GOOD...

SORT OF ☐ (0 points)

ONLY ON SPECIAL OCCASIONS ☐ (0 points)

ALL YEAR LONG ☐ (1 point)

4. S.O.S. STANDS FOR...

SMALL ONION SOUP ☐ (0 points)

SAVE OUR SOULS ☐ (1 point)

SCAREDY ORVILLE SQUIRREL ☐ (1 point)

5.

OBSERVE THIS INKBLOT AND DESCRIBE WHAT YOU SEE.

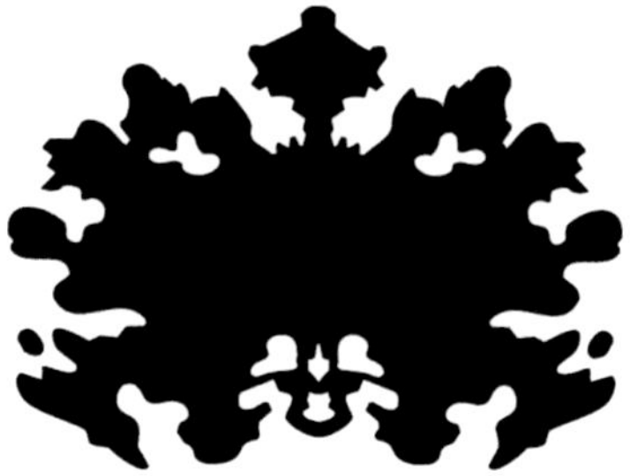

ANSWER: AN INK SPOT THAT NEEDS TO BE SPOT-CLEANED IMMEDIATELY. (1 point)

6.

HAVE YOU BEEN IN CONTACT WITH ANY OF THESE INDIVIDUALS IN THE PAST 12 MONTHS?

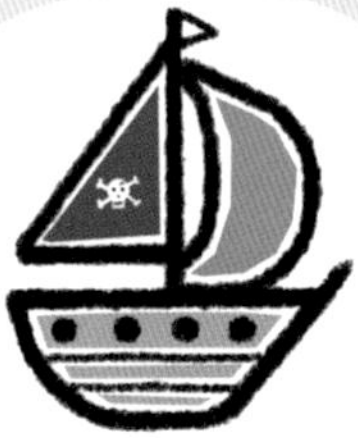

PIRATES

(0 points)

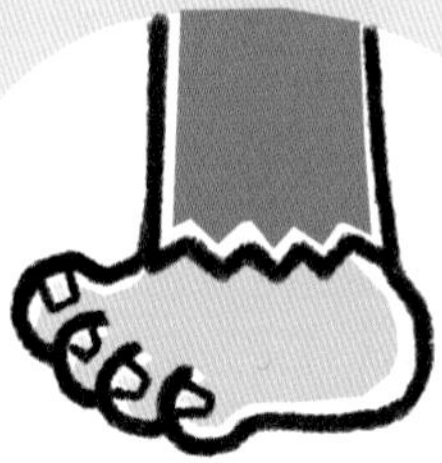

BIGFOOT

(0 points)

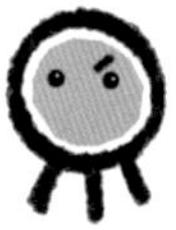

GARY THE GERM

(-87 points)

CONGRATULATIONS!
IF YOUR TOTAL POINTS ARE BETWEEN 1 AND 6, YOU CAN SAFELY PROCEED TO THE NEXT PAGE.

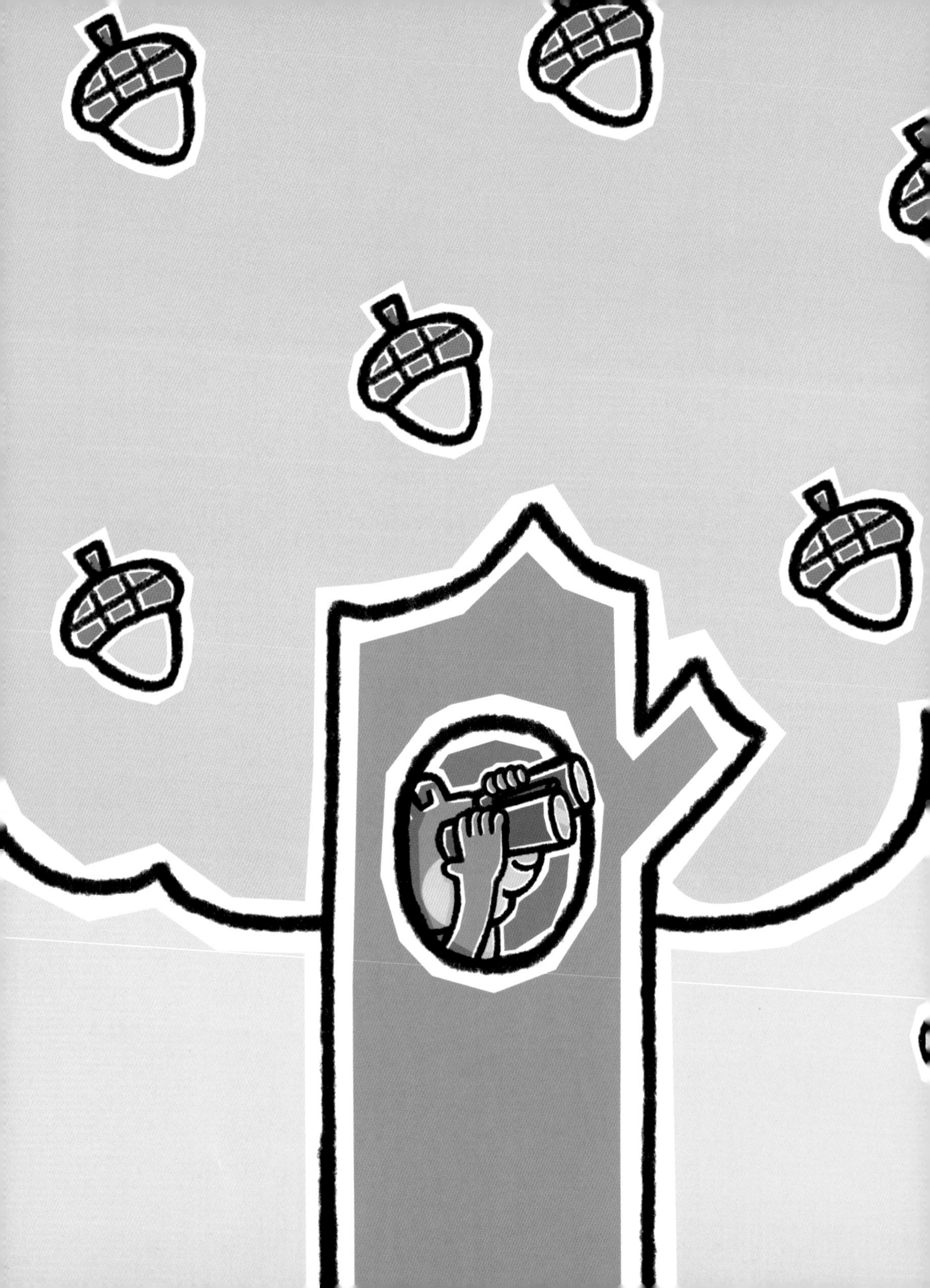

Scaredy Squirrel

In a Nutshell

BY MELANIE WATT

A Stepping Stone Book™

Random House 🏠 New York

FOR: **XAVIER**
(WHO I'M ALWAYS NUTS ABOUT!)

Visit us on the Web! rhcbooks.com

Educators and librarians, for a variety of teaching tools, visit us at RHTeachersLibrarians.com

Library of Congress Cataloging-in-Publication Data
Names: Watt, Melanie, author, illustrator.
Title: Scaredy Squirrel in a nutshell / by Melanie Watt.
Description: First edition. | New York : Random House Children's Books, 2021.
Series: [Scaredy Squirrel ; 1] | Audience: Ages 6–9. | Summary: Scaredy has spent his life defending his tree from UFOs, lumberjacks, mammoths, and more, so when (possibly poison) Ivy the rabbit sends a note he must calculate the risks of friendship.
Identifiers: LCCN 2020032029 (print) | LCCN 2020032030 (ebook) | ISBN 978-0-593-30755-7 (hardcover) | ISBN 978-0-593-30756-4 (lib. bdg.) | ISBN 978-0-593-30757-1 (ebook)
Subjects: CYAC: Fear—Fiction. | Squirrels—Fiction. | Rabbits—Fiction. | Friendship—Fiction.
Classification: LCC PZ7.W3323 Sc 2021 (print) | LCC PZ7.W3323 (ebook) | DDC [E]—dc23

MANUFACTURED IN CHINA
10 9 8 7 6 5 4 3 2 1 First Edition

NUTTY CONTENTS

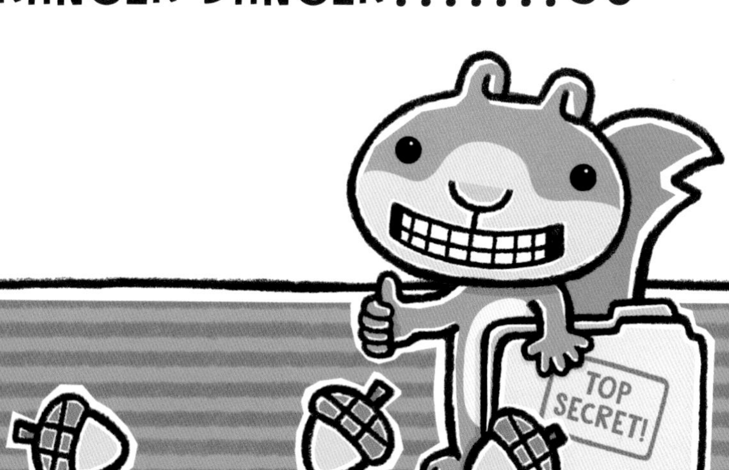
TOP SECRET!

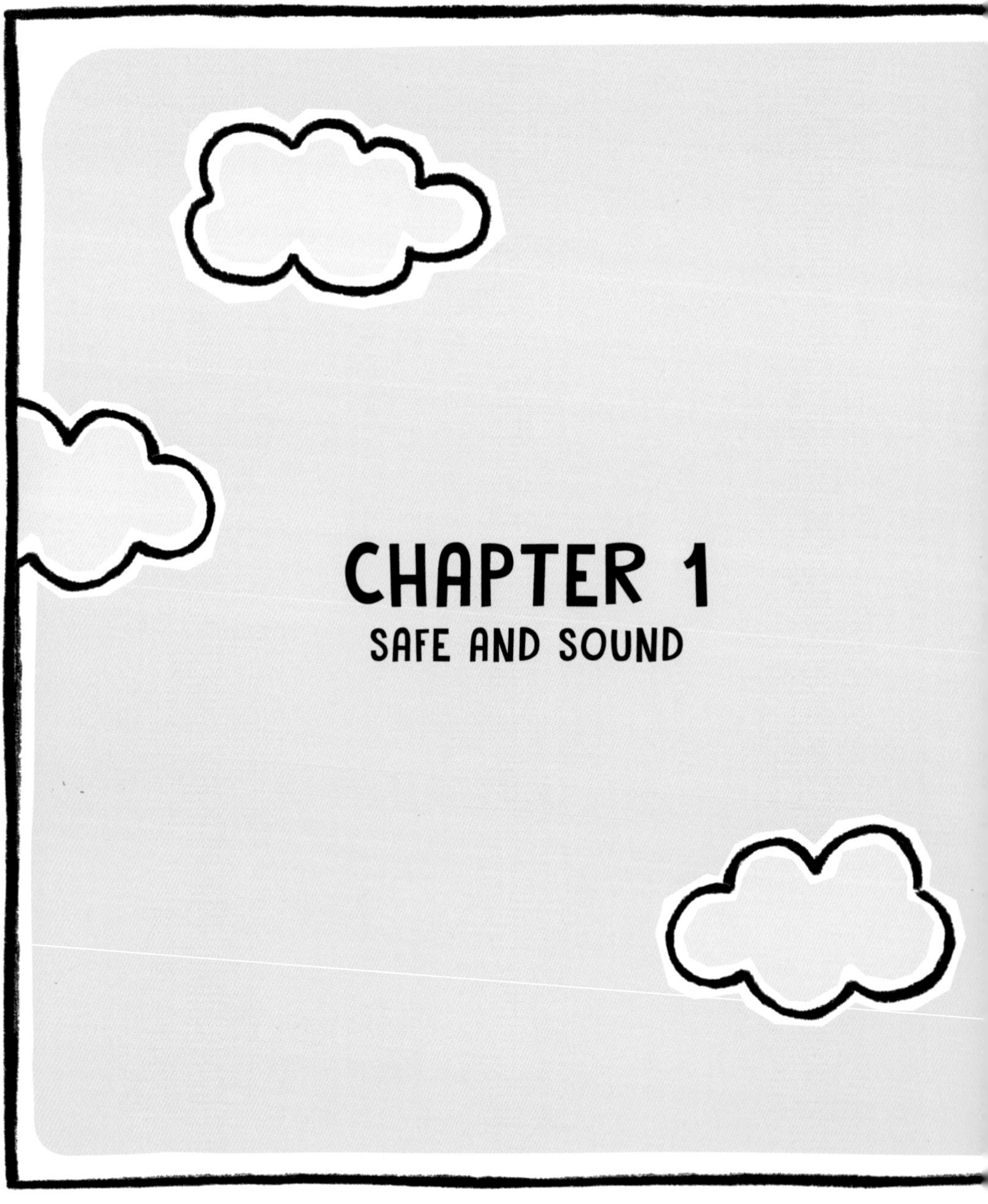

CHAPTER 1
SAFE AND SOUND

SCAREDY SQUIRREL
WATCHES OVER HIS
NUT TREE.

9

A FEW TRESPASSERS
SCAREDY SQUIRREL
IS AFRAID COULD
DROP BY:

MUST
UPROOT
TREE!

MAMMOTHS

MUST
POKE HOLES
IN TREE!

WOODPECKERS

ALIENS

LUMBERJACKS

CATS

TERMITES

11

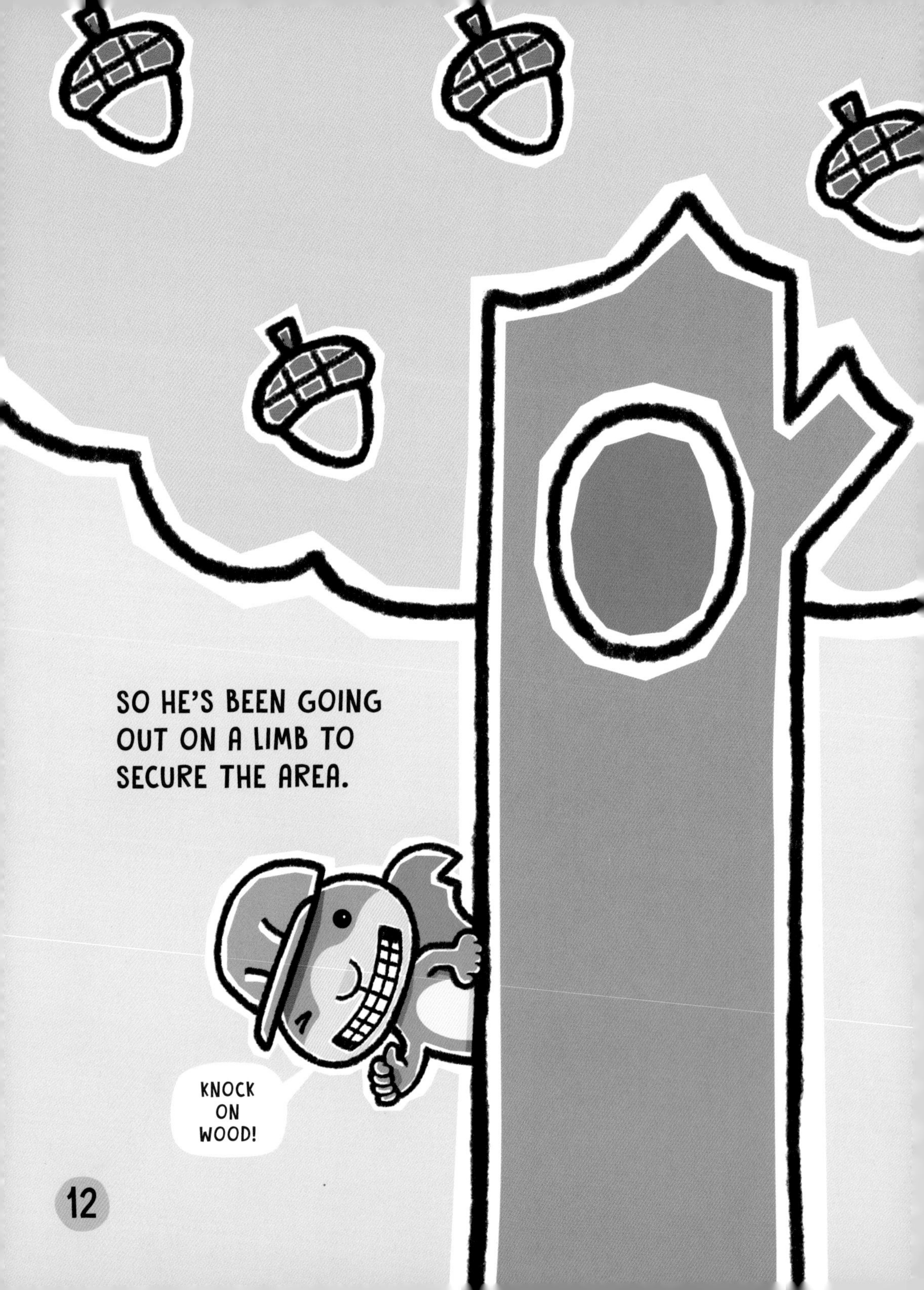
SO HE'S BEEN GOING OUT ON A LIMB TO SECURE THE AREA.
KNOCK ON WOOD!

THIS PAGE IS BLANK FOR SUPERSTITIOUS REASONS.

MUST
JINX
TREE!

13

SCAREDY SQUIRREL BEGAN PROTECTING
HIS NUT TREE AT AN EARLY AGE.

WARNING!
CUTE FACTOR MIGHT BE
OVERWHELMING FOR SOME.

WOODEN
TRAIN
SIDETRACKS
TERMITES

TRAFFIC CONE
FENDS OFF
ALIENS

15

AS SCAREDY'S NUT TREE GREW, SO DID HIS SAFETY MEASURES.

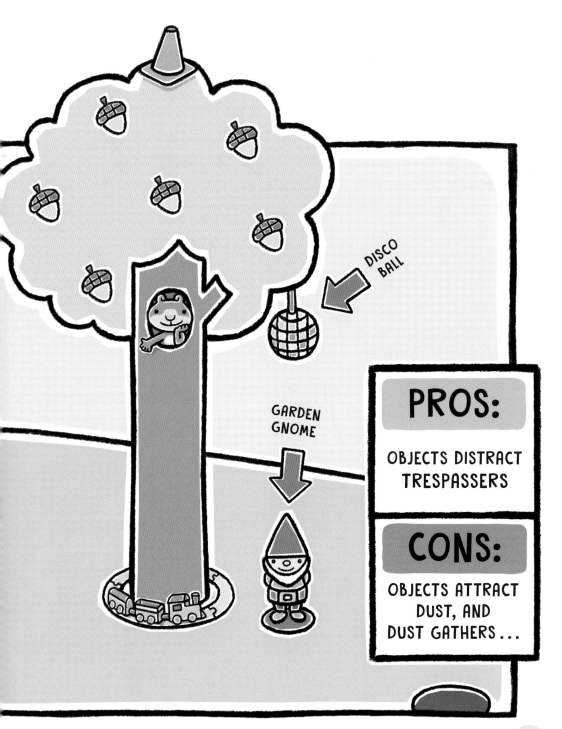

DISCO BALL

GARDEN GNOME

PROS:
OBJECTS DISTRACT TRESPASSERS

CONS:
OBJECTS ATTRACT DUST, AND DUST GATHERS...

17

DUST BUNNIES
(ACCORDING TO SCAREDY SQUIRREL)

MUST SPREAD DUST AROUND TREE!

SIGNALS A BUNCH OF DUSTY SIBLINGS WITH ANTENNAE

DIGS BURROWS

SNEEZES

ADORABLE POM-POM TAIL

97% SURE THEY'RE PALS WITH GARY

 LUCKILY, SCAREDY KNOWS HOW TO KEEP THINGS CLEAN WITH A...

SCUBA MASK

DUST-REPELLENT SUIT

PAIR OF
RUBBER GLOVES

VACUUM

SCAREDY SQUIRREL
VACUUMS...

PLAID
SALE!!!

(IN THE CITY)

AND VACUUMS...

AND VACUUMS...

WHEN SUDDENLY...

THE VACUUM CLOGS!

21

A FEW ITEMS THAT COULD BE AT THE BOTTOM OF THIS:

A. WOOL

B. FEATHERS

C. BOLTS AND SCREWS

D. MUSTACHES

E. HAIRBALLS

F. WOOD CHIPS

HE MUST UNCLOG
THIS VACUUM BEFORE
THE DUST SETTLES IN!

SCAREDY'S SWIFT UNCLOGGING PLAN

STEP 1: PANIC

STEP 2: SLIDE DOWN VACUUM

STEP 3: LIFT VACUUM NOZZLE

STEP 4: UNCLOG IT WITH PLUNGER

STEP 5: HURRY BACK UP TREE

STEP 6: RESUME VACUUMING

DO NOT STEP ON GROUND

MAYDAY!
Shedding woolly mammoths like to scratch their behinds on icy, snow-covered trees!

MOVE FAST!
Lumberjacks may be twirling their mustaches near tempting sign.

PLAID SALE!!!

(IN THE CITY)

LOOK OUT!
Aliens want to beam up everything! If spaceship hovers too long, loose bolts, nuts and screws can drop to the ground!

I AM HERE.

ALERT!
Woodpeckers cannot stand the glare of mirrors. If they come a-knocking, feathers will fly!

CAREFUL!
Wooden train is packed with wood chips and dizzy termites.

REMEMBER!
This sturdy security guard is on duty!

DANGER!
Stepping on a hairball can lead to a mushy mess!

CLOG IS IN HERE.

ACHOO!

NOTE TO SELF: IF ALL ELSE FAILS, PLAY DEAD FOR 2 HOURS, THEN DUST YOURSELF OFF!

AS PLANNED,
SCAREDY SLIDES
DOWN THE VACUUM.

THEN HE CAREFULLY
LIFTS UP THE NOZZLE...

AND DISCOVERS SOMETHING MORE TERRIFYING
THAN HE HAD EVER IMAGINED...

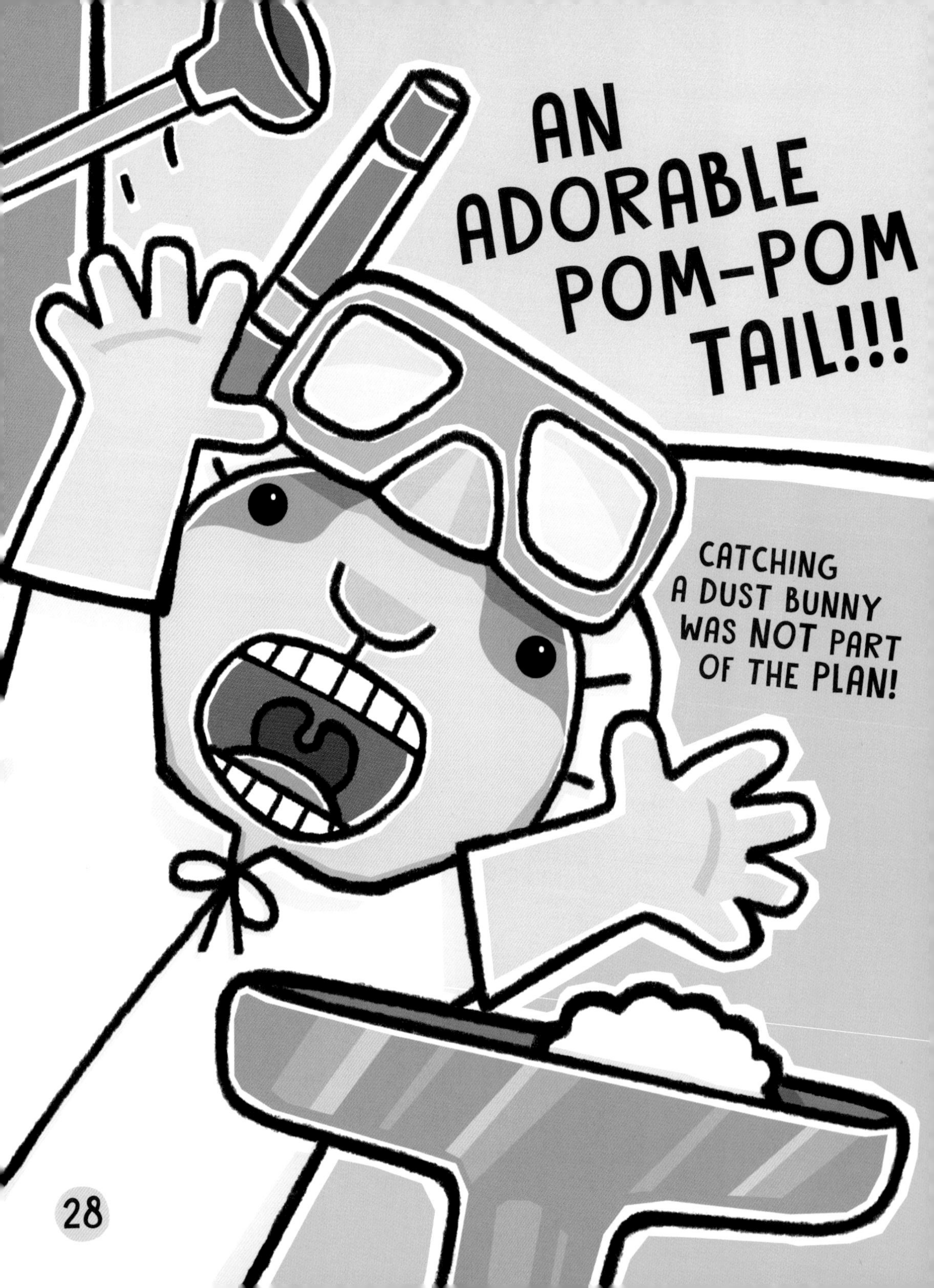
AN ADORABLE POM-POM TAIL!!!
CATCHING A DUST BUNNY WAS NOT PART OF THE PLAN!

SCAREDY RACES BACK UP THE TREE
AND KNOCKS DOWN THE VACUUM...

WHICH KNOCKS OFF THE
DISCO BALL...

WHICH KNOCKS THE GNOME...

WHICH KNOCKS INTO THE TREE...

AND KNOCKS OUT EVERY SINGLE NUT!

30

SCAREDY SQUIRREL PANICS AND...

PLAYS DEAD.

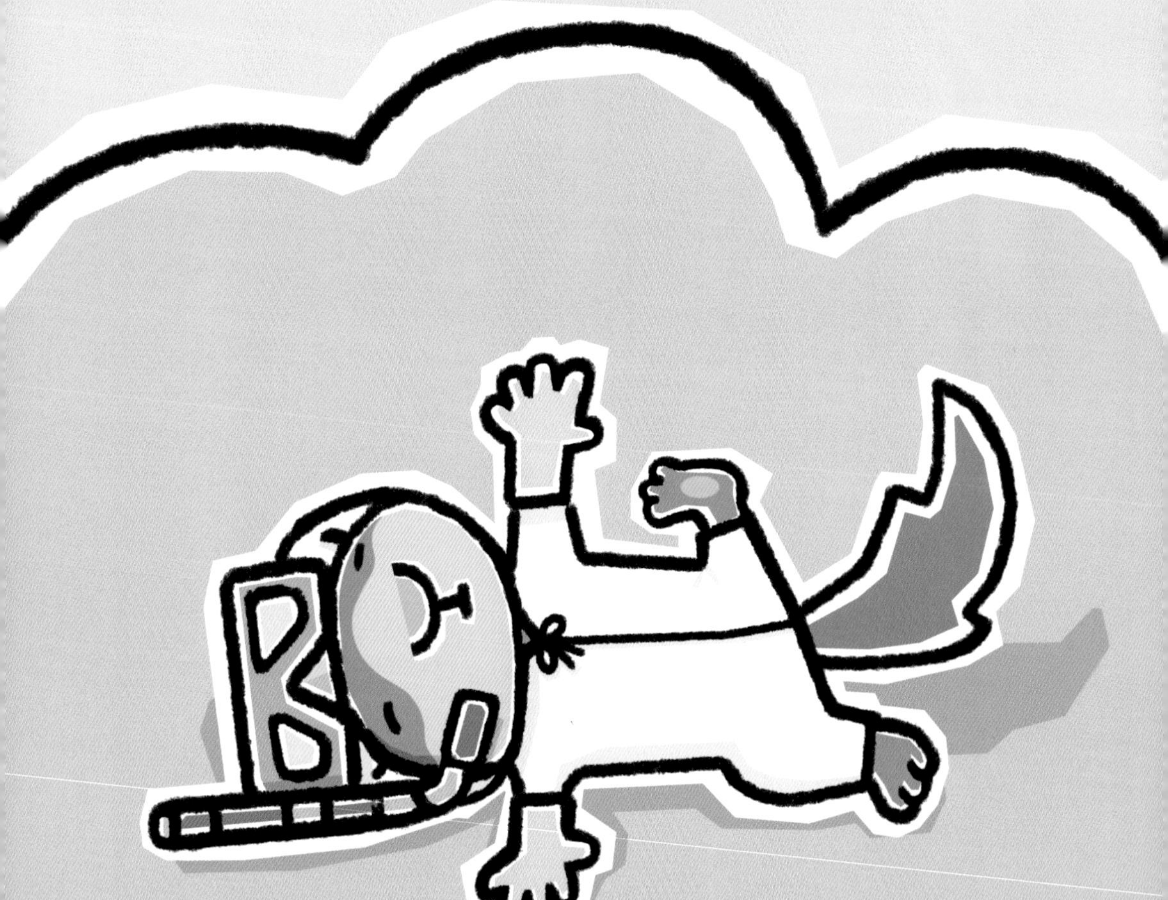

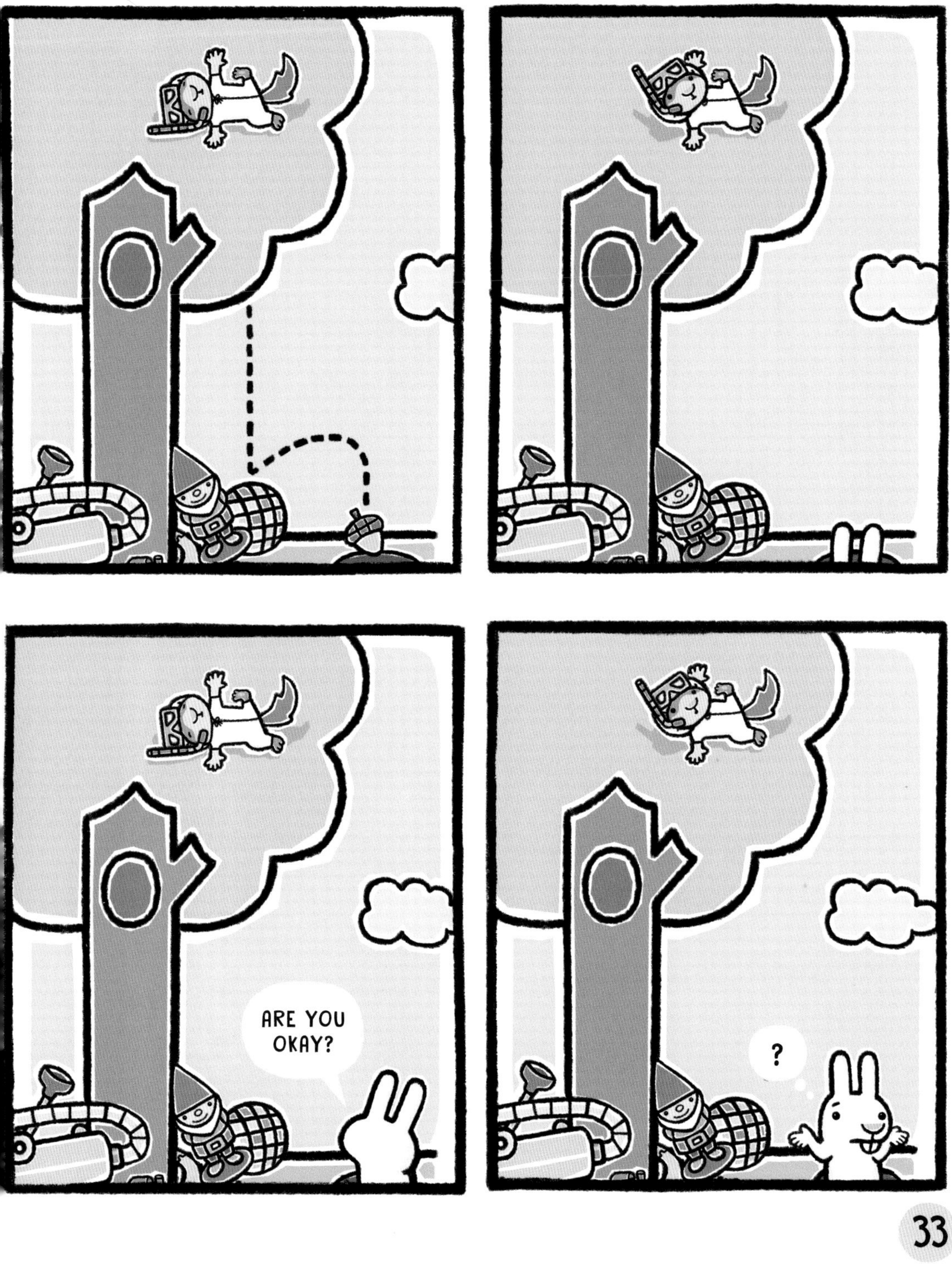
ARE YOU OKAY?
?

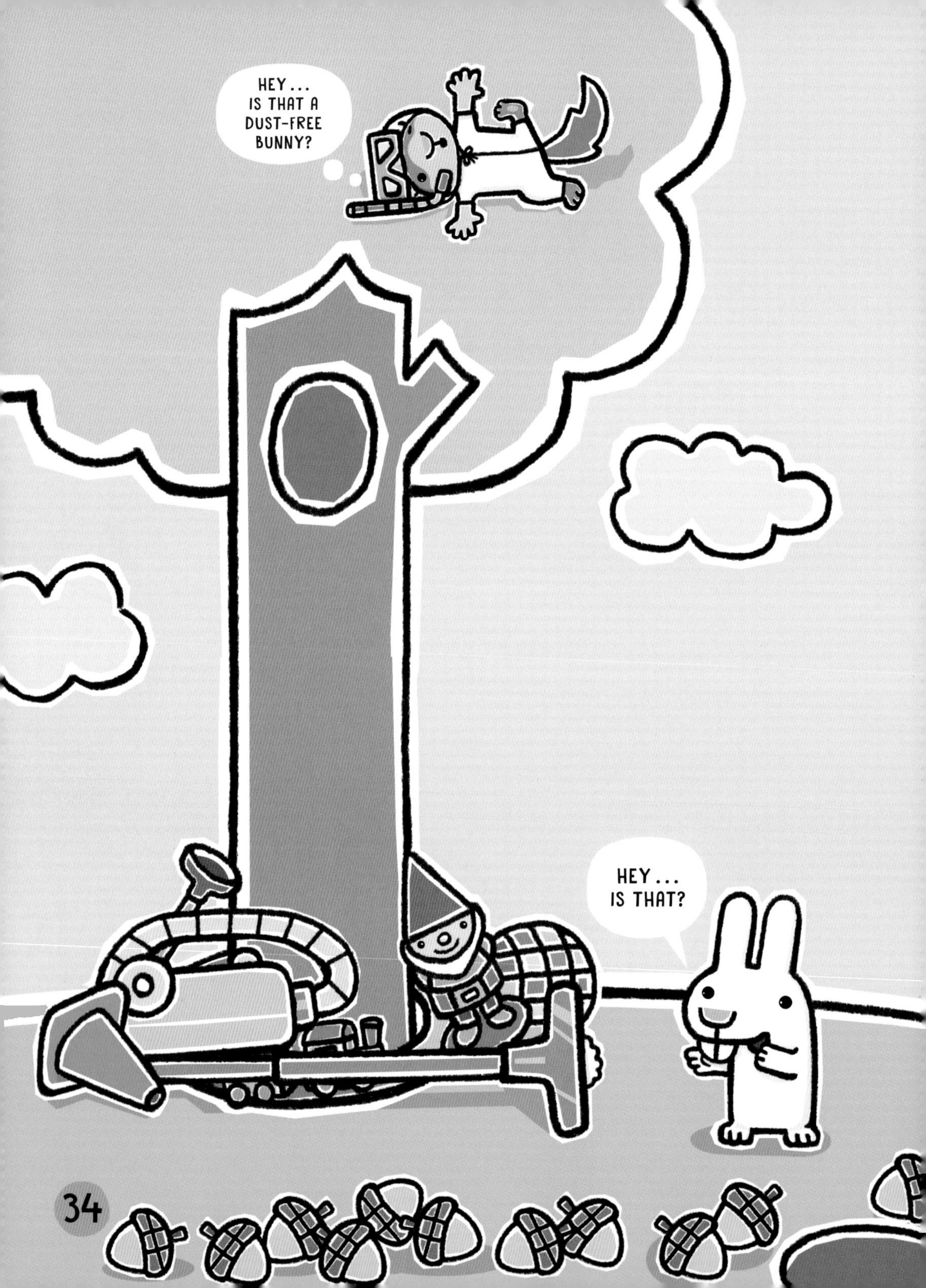
HEY...
IS THAT A
DUST-FREE
BUNNY?
HEY...
IS THAT?

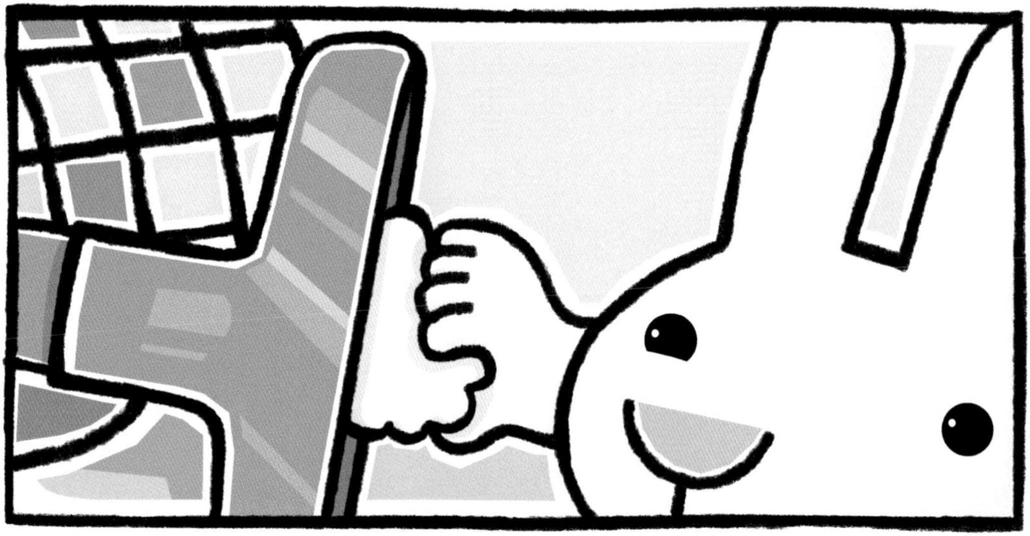

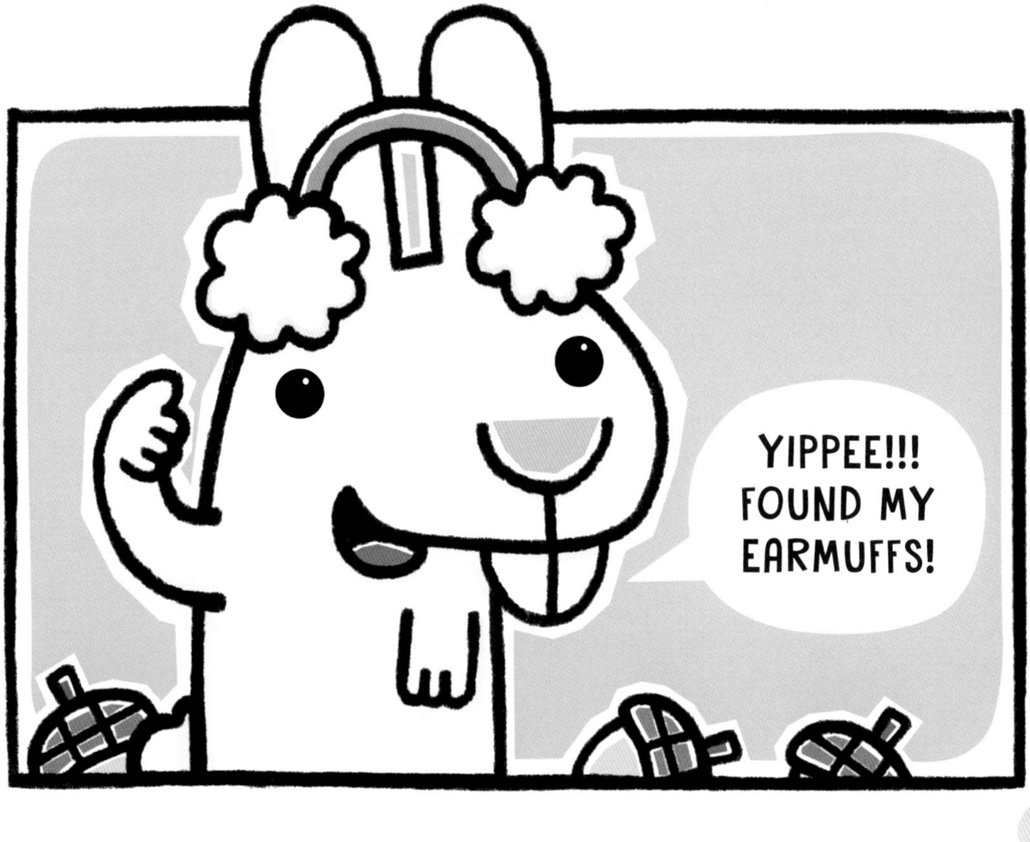
YIPPEE!!!
FOUND MY
EARMUFFS!

2 HOURS LATER...

CHAPTER 2
OUT AND ABOUT

SCAREDY SQUIRREL
WANTS TO EAT A NUT.

BUT TO GET A NUT,
HE MUST SET FOOT ON
DANGEROUS GROUND.

38

 A FEW POSSIBLE RUN-INS THAT MAKE THIS A RISKY MOVE:

ROCKS

CACTI

PUDDLES

BURROWS AND...

THE BUNNY
(ACCORDING TO SCAREDY SQUIRREL)

Scaredy's TO-DO List:

☑ Wait an entire year for new nuts to grow in.

Fall

Summer

Winter

Spring

☑ In the meantime, order takeout!

A FEW SNACKS ON SCAREDY'S DINING PLAN:

THE EARLY SQUIRREL SPECIAL!

NUT OVER EASY

NO HOT PEPPERS!

NUT TACO

GRILLED AT A SAFE DISTANCE!

NUT KEBAB

BEST INVENTION SINCE SLICED ALMONDS!

NUT SANDWICH

FAST AND EASY FOR RODENTS WHO ARE NEVER ON THE GO!

NUT SMOOTHIE

PLEASING TO THE EYE AND MOUTH!

NUT SUSHI

A HEALTHY CHOICE!

NUT SALAD

HELLO, MAY I PLACE AN ORDER, PLEASE?

NUTTY FOOD TRUCK
SORRY! WE ARE CLOSED TODAY.
FLAT TIRE

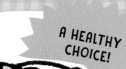

FORTUNATELY,
THIS SQUIRREL ALWAYS
HAS A PLAN B . . .

PLAN B:

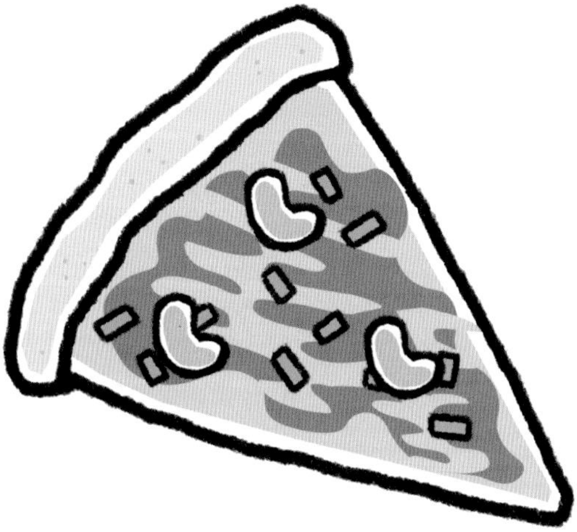

PIZZA

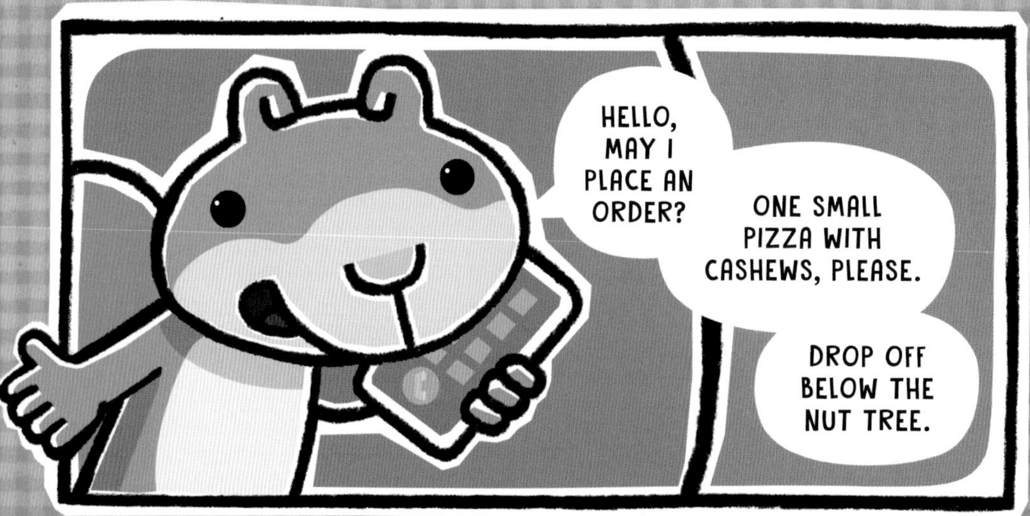

HELLO, MAY I PLACE AN ORDER?
ONE SMALL PIZZA WITH CASHEWS, PLEASE.
DROP OFF BELOW THE NUT TREE.

31 MINUTES LATER...

HMMM. NUT TREE? WHERE?

PIZZA

SCAREDY'S DELIVERY GETS DROPPED OFF...

IN THE WRONG SPOT!

PILE OF NUTS, CLOSE ENOUGH!

PLAID SALE, HERE I COME!

PIZZA

ANY WAY YOU SLICE IT, SCAREDY WILL HAVE TO SET FOOT ON THE GROUND. THIS IS RISKY ON A WHOLE OTHER LEVEL!

SCAREDY'S GROUND-LEVEL GET-UP:

SAFETY HELMET

T. REX GRABBER TOOL

ELBOW PADS

KNEE PADS

STILTS

DO NOT STEP ON GROUND

1. MARCH TOWARD THE PIZZA BOX
2. OPEN BOX WITH GRABBER TOOL
3. GRAB A SLICE WITH GRABBER TOOL
4. HURRY BACK UP TREE, EAT SLICE
5. REPEAT STEPS UNTIL BOX IS EMPTY

NOTE TO SELF: IF IT ALL FALLS FLAT, PLAY DEAD!

SCAREDY STARTS MARCHING...

HE APPROACHES THE PIZZA...

AND LEANS IN TO OPEN THE BOX WHEN...

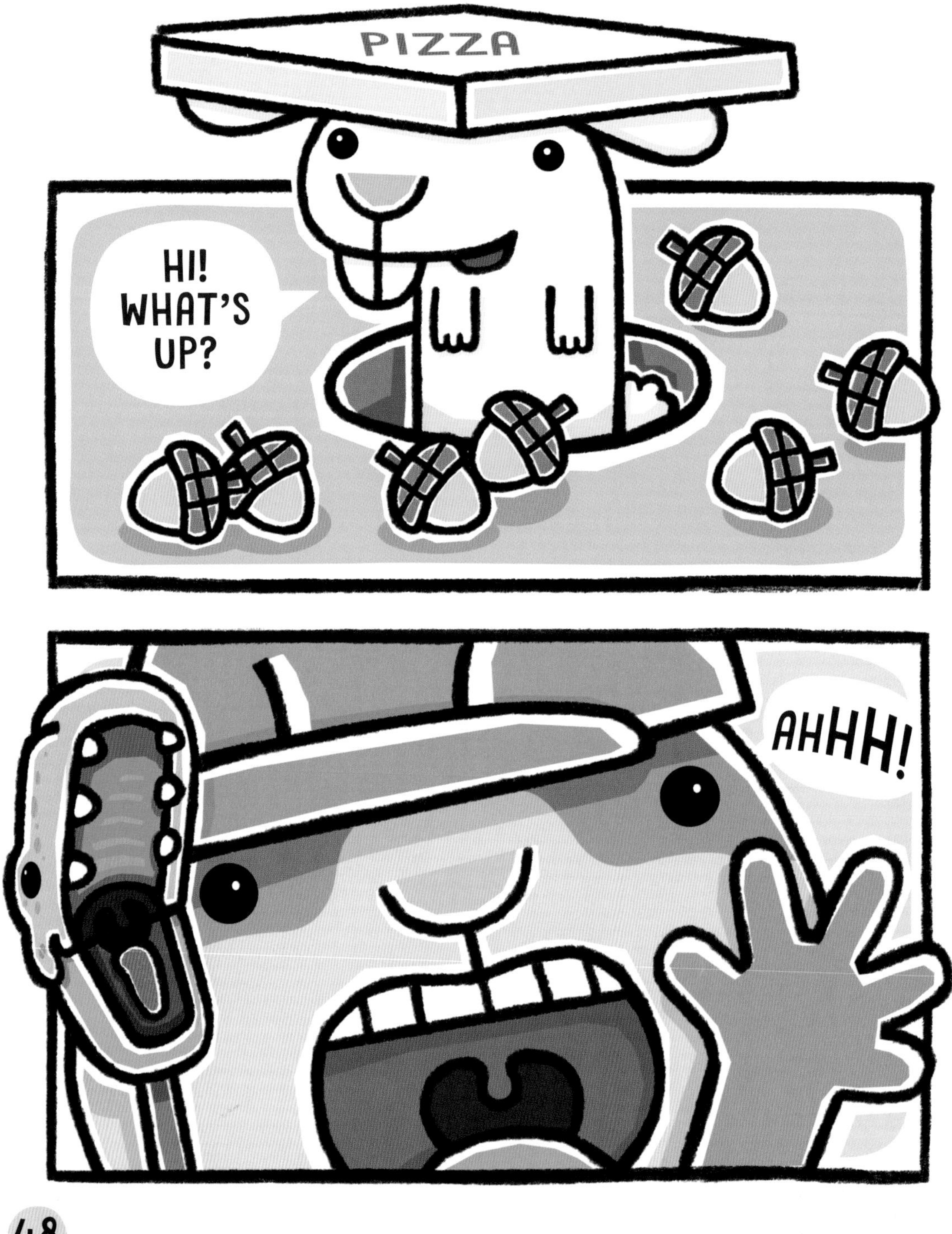
PIZZA
HI! WHAT'S UP?
AHHH!

SCAREDY SCRAMBLES TO SAFETY AND PLAYS DEAD.

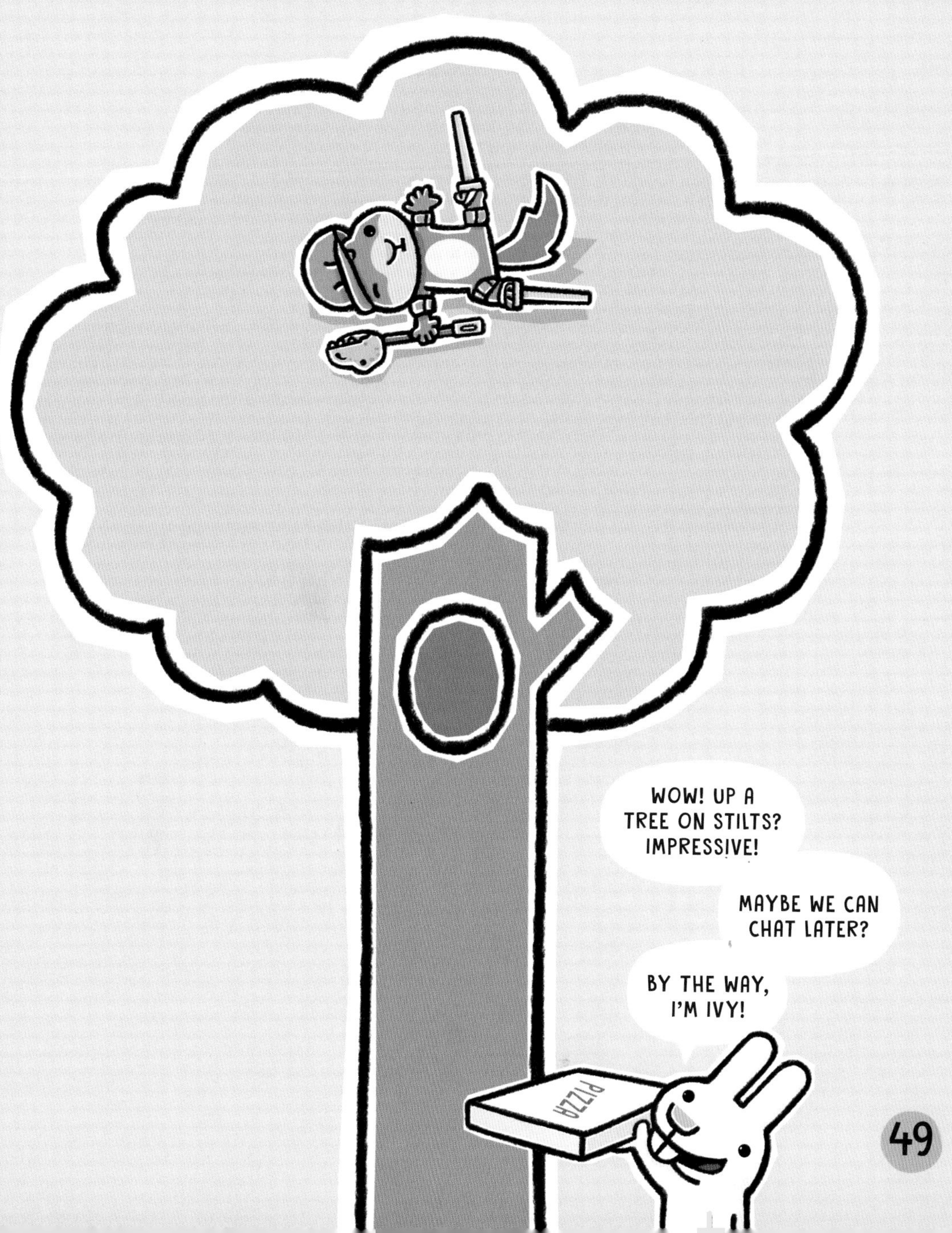
WOW! UP A TREE ON STILTS? IMPRESSIVE!
MAYBE WE CAN CHAT LATER?
BY THE WAY, I'M IVY!
PIZZA

CHAPTER 3
STRANGER DANGER

SCAREDY SQUIRREL
IS HUNGRY FOR
ANSWERS.

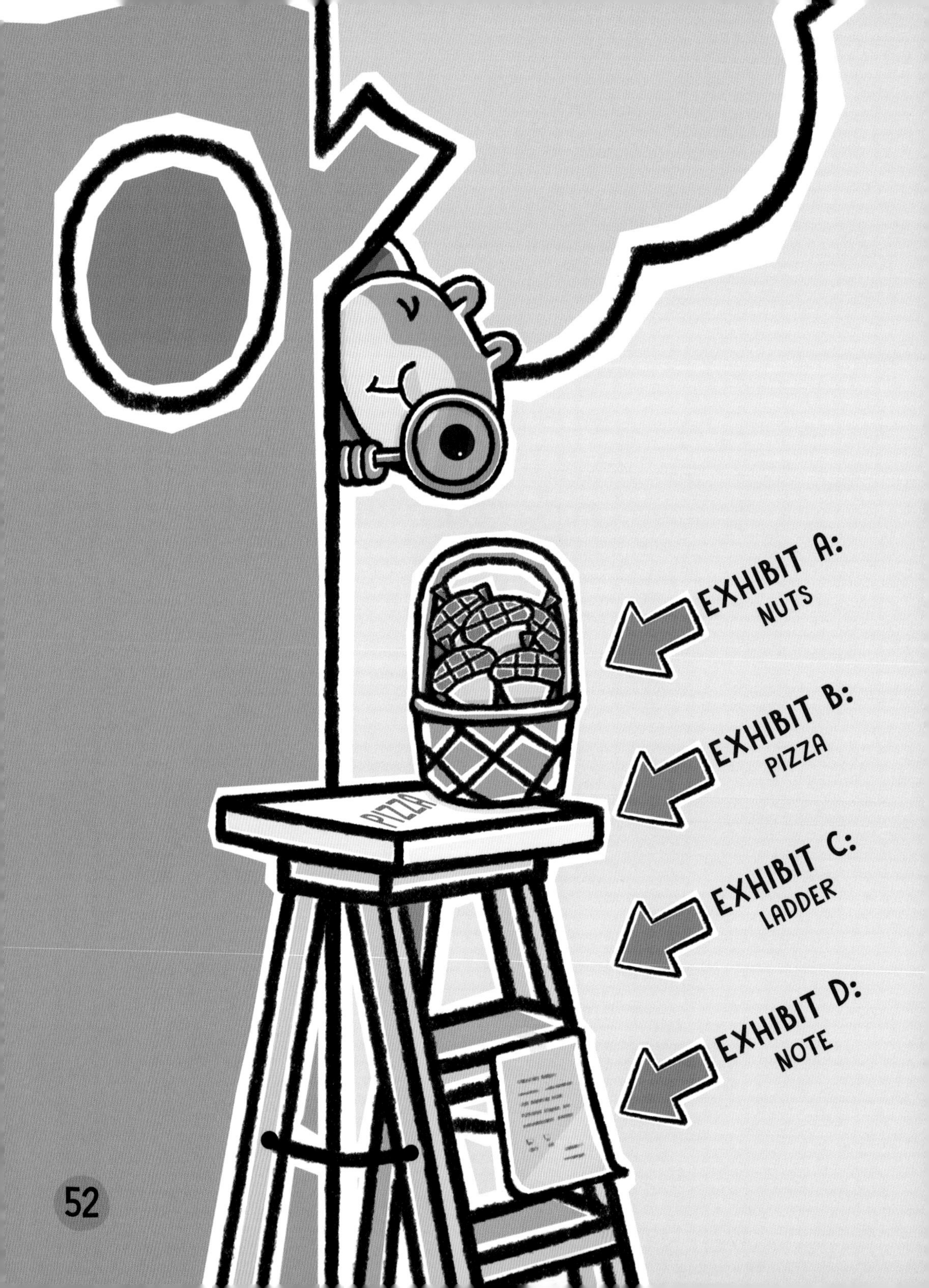
EXHIBIT A:
NUTS
EXHIBIT B:
PIZZA
PIZZA
EXHIBIT C:
LADDER
EXHIBIT D:
NOTE

TO AVOID PAPER CUTS, SCAREDY PUTS ON HIS OVEN MITTS.

Hi, up there. Sorry if I scared you earlier. Maybe we can meet halfway?

☐ Yes ☐ No

Ivy
(your friendly neighbor)

SCAREDY SQUIRREL IS STUMPED. HE MUST CALCULATE THE RISKS BEFORE HE CAN ANSWER IVY.

RISKS:

1. Ivy might be
poisonous!
(name makes me itchy)

DANGER!

2. Ivy might really be
Gary in disguise!

HEE! HEE! HEE! 'TWAS ME ALL ALONG!

3. Ivy might be a
spy searching
for my classified
information!

TOP SECRET!

GOTCHA, SQUIRREL!

4. Ivy and I might
have **nothing**
in common!!!

AWKWARD!

BENEFITS:

1. Ivy is NOT a dust bunny.

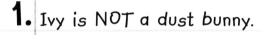

2. Ivy is kind to my tree.

I ♥🌳

3. Ivy is friendly to me.

LET'S CHAT!

4. Ivy unclogs vacuums.

5. Ivy is helpful.

PIZZA

6. Ivy smiles.

7. Ivy is peaceful.

8. Ivy has impeccable handwriting!
(a rare skill nowadays)

AFTER CAREFUL THOUGHT,
SCAREDY CONCLUDES THAT THE
REALISTIC BENEFITS OUTWEIGH
THE UNLIKELY RISKS.

IN A NUTSHELL:
IVY=SAFE

SCAREDY HANDS
OVER HIS ANSWER.

OKAY...
A BIT STRANGE.
BUT WORKS
FOR ME!

Yes

Let's meet
halfway and
split a pizza
at half
past 5!

A FEW LAST-MINUTE DETAILS SCAREDY MUST HANDLE BEFORE 5:30 P.M.:

MEASURING TAPE

NAME TAGS

TOOTHPASTE

RADIO

HAND SANITIZER

NAPKINS

4:52 P.M. SCAREDY MEASURES THE HALFWAY SPOT.

5:07 P.M. HE PREPARES AN ID VERIFICATION TEST.

HELLO MY NAME IS

HELLO MY NAME IS

HELLO MY NAME IS Ivy

5:09 P.M. HE BRUSHES HIS TEETH.

5:12 P.M. HE PLAYS ELEVATOR MUSIC AND WAITS.

SERIOUSLY?

5:30 P.M. SCAREDY AND IVY FINALLY MEET FACE-TO-FACE (SORT OF).

HELLO! MY NAME IS SCAREDY SQUIRREL. PLEASE PICK THE NAME TAG THAT BEST SUITS YOU!

HELLO MY NAME IS Poison Ivy

Gary

Ivy

Spy

HI, SCARE-DY! THAT EXPLAINS A LOT!

IVY! MAY I OFFER YOU A SPRITZ OF HAND SANITIZER, 9 NAPKINS AND A SLICE OF PIZZA?

SURE!

PIZZA

HELLO MY NAME IS Ivy

HELLO MY NAME IS Scaredy

SCAREDY EAGERLY OPENS THE BOX...

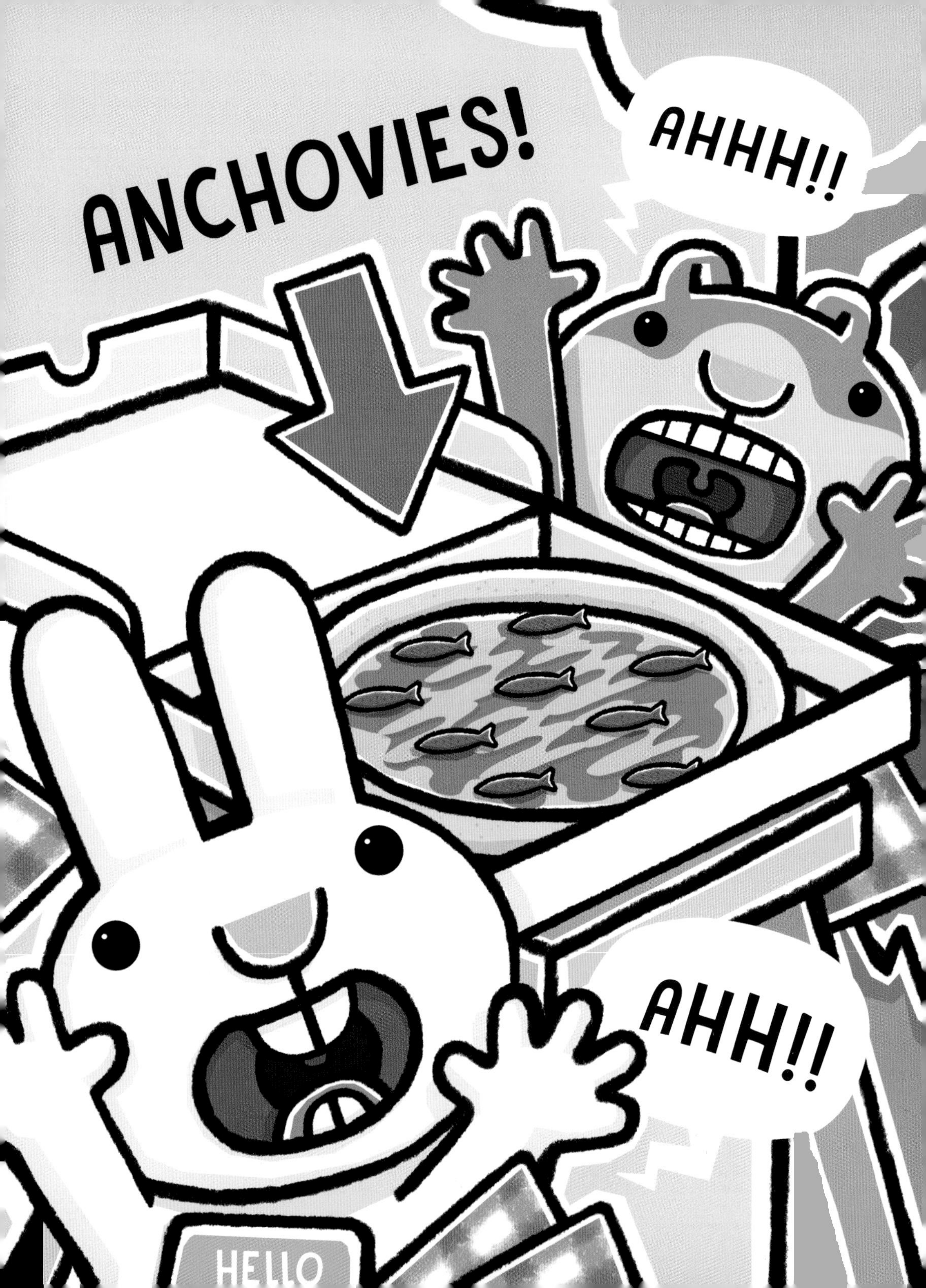
ANCHOVIES!
AHHHH!!
AHH!!
HELLO

2 MINUTES LATER, THEY REALIZE...

WE HAVE SOMETHING IN COMMON!!!

I'M SCARED OF ANCHOVIES!

I'M SCARED OF ANCHOVIES TOO!

ARE YOU SCARED OF SPAGHETTI?

NO... WHY?

IT TANGLES!

I LOVE POPCORN! DO YOU?

IT POPS! TOO SCARY!!

WHAT ABOUT BEETS?

STAINS.

BUT I LOVE NUTS!

PLEASE TELL ME YOU'RE NOT AFRAID OF CARROTS.

OF COURSE NOT! THAT WOULD BE SILLY!

OKAY, SO THEY DON'T HAVE THAT MUCH IN COMMON.
BUT SCAREDY IS STILL GLAD HE MET A NEW FRIEND!

SCAREDY AND IVY HAVE A PICNIC...

THEY CHAT...

WHEN I'M NOT IN MY BURROW, I GARDEN AND ENJOY READING ALL SORTS OF BOOKS!

WHEN I'M NOT IN MY NUT TREE...I PANIC. I ENJOY READING WARNING SIGNS AND EXPIRATION DATES!

AND THEY WATCH THE SUNSET.

...PIZZA!!!
WE FORGOT THE PIZZA! IVY! LET'S HURRY UP AND CATAPULT IT OUT INTO SPACE BEFORE IT ATTRACTS A HERD OF HUNGRY ANCHOVY-LOVING FLAMINGOS!!

OR...
WE COULD JUST CALL MY FRIEND TIM!

[crickets chirping]

TIM LOVES ANCHOVIES! HE ADORES TREES! DON'T WORRY, SCAREDY. YOU'LL BOTH GET ALONG SO WELL!!!

TIM IS SHORT FOR TIMOTHY, RIGHT?

UH... NOT EXACTLY?

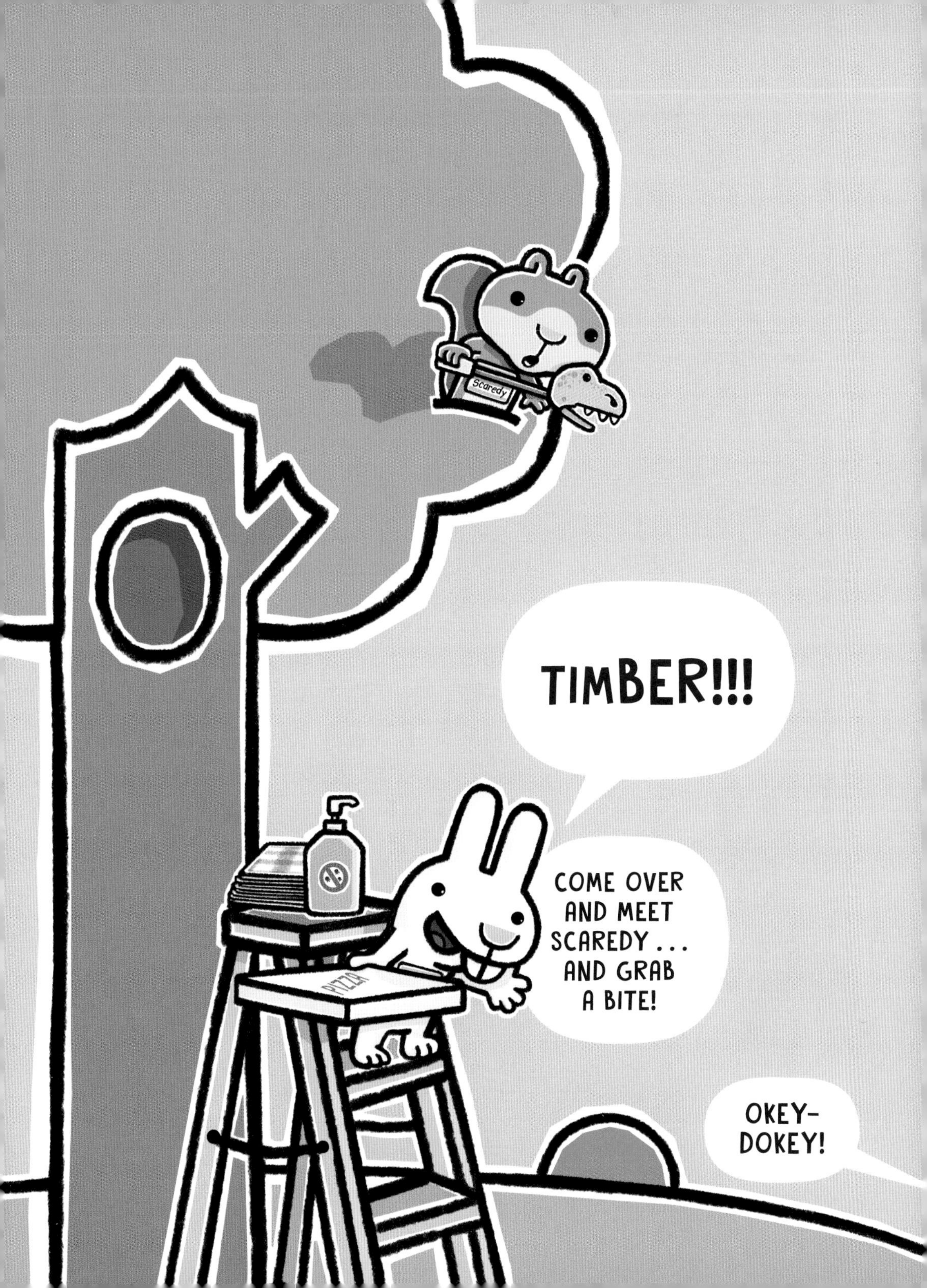
Scaredy
TIMBER!!!
COME OVER AND MEET SCAREDY . . . AND GRAB A BITE!
PIZZA
OKEY-DOKEY!

TIMBER

(ACCORDING TO SCAREDY SQUIRREL)

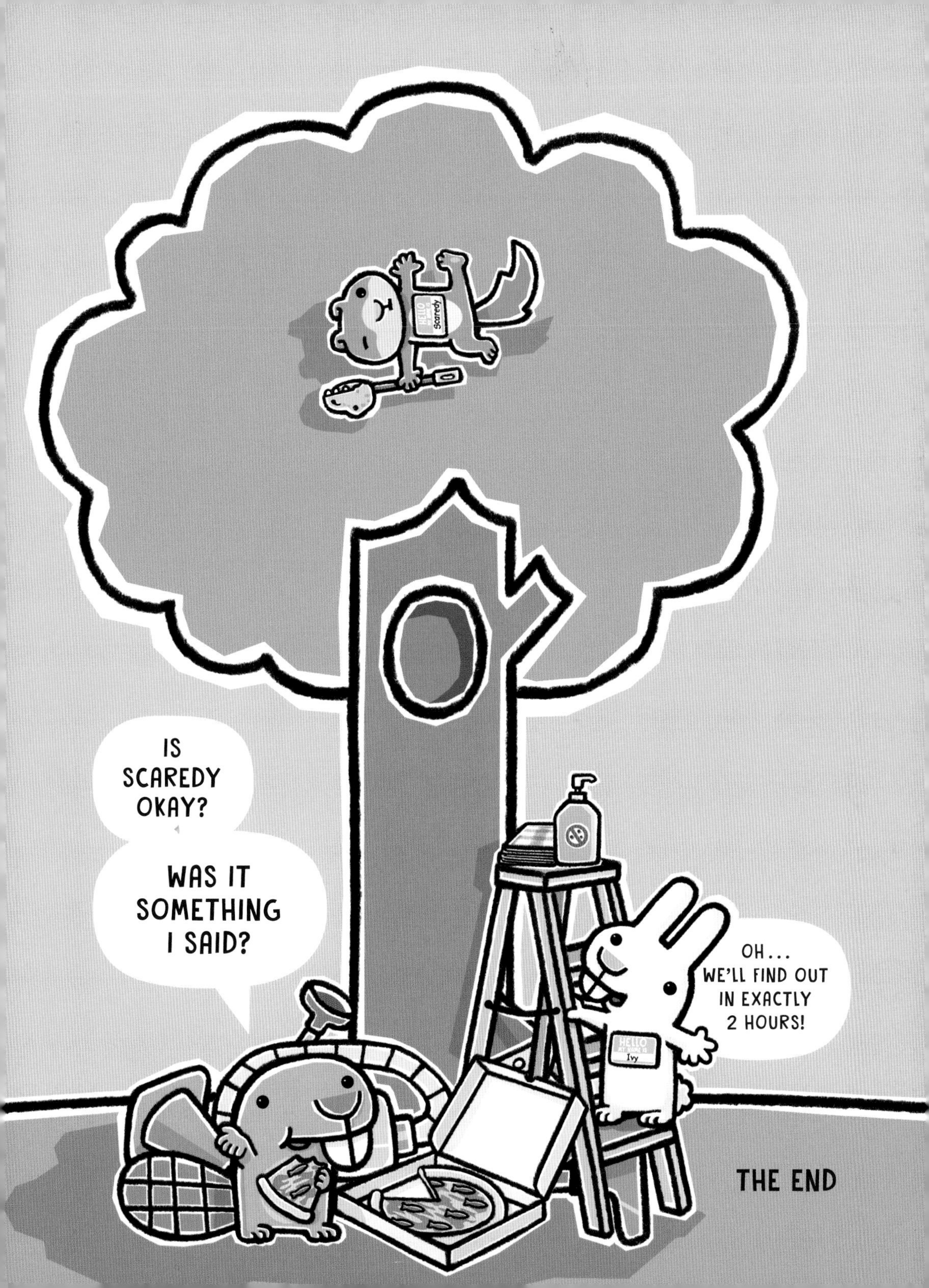

Scaredy
IS SCAREDY OKAY?
WAS IT SOMETHING I SAID?
OH... WE'LL FIND OUT IN EXACTLY 2 HOURS!
Ivy
THE END

FAQ

(FREQUENTLY ASKED QUESTIONS)

Q1 **SCAREDY, WILL YOU BE BACK WITH NEW NUTTY ADVENTURES?**

S.O.S.: YES!!! I have plenty to be afraid of ... like Vikings, clams, yetis, bookworms and Gary.

MUST POKE SQUIRREL!

Q2 **SCAREDY, WHO'S THIS GARY YOU KEEP MENTIONING?**

S.O.S.: A clingy germ rival who dates from waaay back.

GA-GA GRRR!

Q3 **WHERE CAN I FIND A SCAREDY SQUIRREL BOBBLEHEAD?**

S.O.S.: Hopefully, nowhere!!!
Just the thought makes me dizzy!

SORRY TO INTERRUPT, BUT IS THERE ANY PIZZA LEFT?

Q4 **SCAREDY, WHY AREN'T YOU LIKE A TYPICAL TREE SQUIRREL?**

S.O.S.: Because I'm not a typical tree squirrel — I'm atypical!
And that's what makes my adventures so incredibly fun!

Q5 **SCAREDY, CAN YOU LIST ALL OF YOUR PICTURE BOOKS?**

S.O.S.:
- Scaredy Squirrel
- Scaredy Squirrel Makes a Friend
- Scaredy Squirrel at the Beach
- Scaredy Squirrel at Night
- Scaredy Squirrel Has a Birthday Party
- Scaredy Squirrel Goes Camping
...and more to come!

WATCH OUT FOR PAPER CUTS!